Put Beginning Readers on the Right Track with
ALL ABOARD READING™

The All Aboard Reading series is especially designed for beginning readers. Written by noted authors and illustrated in full color, these are books that children really want to read—books to excite their imagination, expand their interests, make them laugh, and support their feelings. With fiction and nonfiction stories that are high interest and curriculum-related, All Aboard Reading books offer something for every young reader. And with four different reading levels, the All Aboard Reading series lets you choose which books are most appropriate for your children and their growing abilities.

Picture Readers
Picture Readers have super-simple texts, with many nouns appearing as rebus pictures. At the end of each book are 24 flash cards—on one side is a rebus picture; on the other side is the written-out word.

Station Stop 1
Station Stop 1 books are best for children who have just begun to read. Simple words and big type make these early reading experiences more comfortable. Picture clues help children to figure out the words on the page. Lots of repetition throughout the text helps children to predict the next word or phrase—an essential step in developing word recognition.

Station Stop 2
Station Stop 2 books are written specifically for children who are reading with help. Short sentences make it easier for early readers to understand what they are reading. Simple plots and simple dialogue help children with reading comprehension.

Station Stop 3
Station Stop 3 books are perfect for children who are reading alone. With longer text and harder words, these books appeal to children who have mastered basic reading skills. More complex stories captivate children who are ready for more challenging books.

In addition to All Aboard Reading books, look for All Aboard Math Readers™ (fiction stories that teach math concepts children are learning in school); All Aboard Science Readers™ (nonfiction books that explore the most fascinating science topics in age-appropriate language); and All Aboard Poetry Readers™ (funny, rhyming poems for readers of all levels).

All Aboard for happy reading!

GROSSET & DUNLAP
Published by the Penguin Group
Penguin Group (USA) Inc., 375 Hudson Street, New York, New York 10014, USA
Penguin Group (Canada), 90 Eglinton Avenue East, Suite 700, Toronto,
Ontario M4P 2Y3, Canada (a division of Pearson Penguin Canada Inc.)
Penguin Books Ltd., 80 Strand, London WC2R 0RL, England
Penguin Group Ireland, 25 St. Stephen's Green, Dublin 2, Ireland
(a division of Penguin Books Ltd.)
Penguin Group (Australia), 250 Camberwell Road, Camberwell, Victoria 3124,
Australia (a division of Pearson Australia Group Pty. Ltd.)
Penguin Books India Pvt. Ltd., 11 Community Centre, Panchsheel Park,
New Delhi—110 017, India
Penguin Group (NZ), 67 Apollo Drive, Rosedale, North Shore 0632, New Zealand
(a division of Pearson New Zealand Ltd.)
Penguin Books (South Africa) (Pty.) Ltd., 24 Sturdee Avenue,
Rosebank, Johannesburg 2196, South Africa

Penguin Books Ltd., Registered Offices:
80 Strand, London WC2R 0RL, England

Text and design copyright © 2009 Children's Character Books. Copyright © Animalia Productions Pty
Limited and Pacific Film & Television Commission Pty Ltd MMVIII. Published by Grosset & Dunlap,
a division of Penguin Young Readers Group, 345 Hudson Street, New York, New York 10014.
ALL ABOARD READING and GROSSET & DUNLAP are trademarks of Penguin Group (USA) Inc.
Printed in the U.S.A.

Library of Congress Control Number: 2008020853

ISBN 978-0-448-45078-0   10 9 8 7 6 5 4 3 2 1

ANIMALIA

Talent-O-Topia

By Cathy Hapka
Based on the teleplay by Deanna Oliver

Grosset & Dunlap

Melba Micely and Melford Mouse were reporting a breaking news story about the yearly talent show called Animalia's Talent-O-Topia.

"Everybody who wants to be somebody is here to audition," Melford said.

Allegra watched Melford and Melba on her TV at home.
She didn't think she'd have to audition.
She thought she could just show up and get a spot.

The tryouts were taking place
in the Great Library.
Inside, Alex was feeling nervous.
He was going to be
the host of the show.

"What if I go onstage
with broccoli stuck in my teeth?"
he asked Zoe.
She had an easy answer for him.
"Don't eat broccoli," she said.

Allegra knew she was destined
to be a superstar.
She planned to start
her fabulous singing career
by winning the talent contest.

The animals waited their turn to
perform for the judges.
Zoe held her clipboard and pen.
"Everyone has to audition
and should check in with me," she said.

Allegra pushed her way to the
front of the crowd.
"Sorry to make the rest of you
look bad," she said with a smirk.

She thought her audition
was going to be the best.

But when it was Allegra's turn to
try out, she got stage fright!
She rushed off the stage.

Several other Animalians
were waiting to try out.
G'Bubu was up next!

G'Bubu played the drums.
He wowed the judges with his beat.
"I am down with the beat
and up with the G'Bubu.
I say yes, definitely!"
said Erno Elephant.

Then it was Iggy's turn to
play his horn.
The judges liked him, too.
Iggy and G'Bubu were both
in the show!

Meanwhile Zoe guessed
what was wrong with Allegra.
"You didn't rehearse, did you?
And now you can't think of a song."
Zoe tried to help by singing
"Twinkle, Twinkle, Little Star."

"You have a terrible voice,"
Allegra said.
Zoe was annoyed.
"You want to be a star?" Zoe asked.
"Try acting like one."
Allegra gasped.
"You're a genius!" Allegra cried.

Now Allegra was ready to try out.
She went back onstage.
She was ready to wow the judges.
She acted like a star.
Actually, she acted like every star
she had ever seen!

But the judges still weren't sure.
So Allegra finished by singing
"Twinkle, Twinkle, Little Star."
That finally convinced them.
Allegra was in the show!

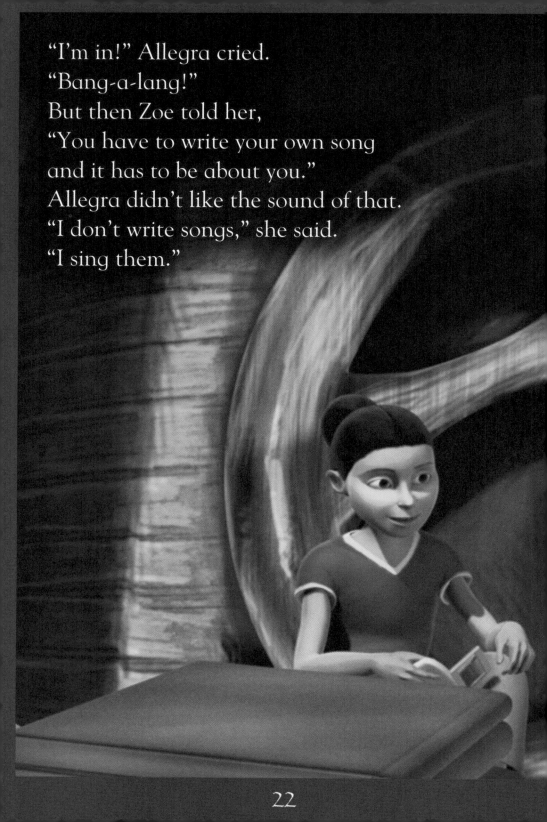

"I'm in!" Allegra cried.
"Bang-a-lang!"
But then Zoe told her,
"You have to write your own song
and it has to be about you."
Allegra didn't like the sound of that.
"I don't write songs," she said.
"I sing them."

"You could help me write a song,"
Allegra told Zoe.
"I don't think I can work with you.
You're difficult," Zoe said.
"Not when you get to know me,"
Allegra said.

"Yeah," Zoe replied.
"Then you're impossible!"
But she agreed to help if she could.
She found some books about music
at the library and
brought them to Allegra's swamp.

They started to write the song.
The title of their song was "Allegra."
Next they needed a first line.
"How about this?" Zoe asked.
"'I'm a star.'"

Allegra thought that was a perfect first
line for her song.
She suggested a second line:
"'Here I are!'" she cried.

Zoe shrugged and typed it in.
Then she thought of a few more lines
and typed those, too.

"What do you think?" she asked.
She showed Allegra the lines.
"I don't like it," Allegra said.

Zoe was annoyed.
Allegra had barely looked
at the lines she had typed.
But she kept trying.
She wrote some different lines.

"The tune is like this—
la-la-la, la-la-la," she sang.
"La-la-la, la-la-la," Allegra sang.
"Right," Zoe said.
"Now try singing the words I wrote."

She showed Allegra the lines.
"La-la-la, la-la-la!"
Allegra sang again.
She refused to sing the lines
Zoe wrote for her.

Now Zoe was getting really annoyed.
"If you don't like the words I wrote,
just say so!" Zoe said.
"I'm out of here. You're impossible!"

"Wait!" Allegra said.
"I can't read, okay?"
Zoe was shocked.

Allegra told Zoe she never
learned to read at school.
She was too busy trying to be popular.
But she could memorize things.
She quoted some poetry.
"That's good, Allegra," Zoe said.
"I couldn't do that.
And I can't sing, either."

"No, you can't," Allegra agreed.
They decided to work as a team
to write a song for the show.
"I've never been on a team before,"
Allegra said.

The night of the talent show arrived.
G'Bubu went first.
He had made up a song that
he played on his drums.

The audience loved it!
So did the judges.
"I love you so very, very
much!" shouted Zee Zebra.

Next it was Iggy's turn.
He played his Snootleblooter.

Everyone loved him, too.
"Iggy, that was hottie-bomb-a-lottie!"
shouted Erno.

Then it was Allegra's turn.
She sang the song that Zoe
had helped her write.

It was called "The Real Me."
It was about staying strong
even when times were rough.

The judges asked her about the words. "I wrote them all myself," Allegra said.

Backstage, Zoe was disappointed.
But then Allegra turned
and smiled at her.
"With Zoe," she added.

After that, the audience voted.
The judges loved everyone,
but they could only pick one winner.

"And now, the moment of truth.
By only two votes,
the best talent in Animalia is . . .
Allegra!" shouted Alex.

Allegra and Zoe were thrilled.
They'd done it—as a team!